The Plan of the Highest Will

For Jayne x

The Plan of the
Highest Will

Love & Light

Estelle Simone Webster

Estelle Simone Webster

*Much love always
to you my friend x*

APEX PUBLISHING LTD

First published in 2006 by

Apex Publishing Ltd

PO Box 7086, Clacton on Sea, Essex, CO15 5WN, England

www.apexpublishing.co.uk

British Library Cataloguing-in-Publication Data
A catalogue record for this book
is available from the British Library

ISBN 1-904444-66-0

Typeset in 12.5pt Gills Sans MT

Production Manager: Chris Cowlin

Cover Design: Andrew Macey

Printed and bound in Great Britain

For my husband, Jonathan

If you believe there's a bridge to heaven
That we climb to a vision of grace,
Just walk a virtuous pathway
Just step a more heavenly pace.
If you understand emotions are waves on a sea
And each breath feeds our spirit by hand,
Where our mind is the soul's campfire
And our journey leaves footprints in the sand.
If you accept we are elements of stars,
Each sign and aspect an invention,
Just live greater with service and purpose,
Discovering the plan of the highest intention.

THE PLAN OF THE HIGHEST WILL

THE GOOD SOLDIER

In a time when things of wonder and magic were real leaves on the tree of life, a story would be told, called The Plan of the Highest Will. It all began when the creator of the first of everything sent a story full of miracles on a journey. This new beginning was merely a breath and its end simply sealed with a contented sigh; a feather, charged with inspiration and purpose, to be released from the wing of the golden phoenix.

It was on a day when a farmer and his cornfield were contented with the heat of the summer's day that the veil of their simple world was pierced, and then slowly torn apart to form a doorway. As the glory of a fairer world slipped through, filling the air with its introduction, a screeching cry rang out. Fearfully expecting the unexplained, the farmer rushed towards his young son lying in the field just ahead, as soaring the illustrious skies of liberty above him was the hot, fast flight of the great golden phoenix, diligently crying over and out the name of the soul who sees with the eye of truth. The father's rescue found a tight grip with his son as they huddled together, caught in a stare of sharp, nervous wonder. The flying messenger's circles of flight came lower and nearer. Suddenly, a swift sweep of one of its giant wings released a crisp, bright feather that darted into the field before them. With this act complete, the phoenix was relinquished of its duty, so it took its glowing wings higher into the skies, far and away, back to the land of every possibility.

As the trance of majesty dissolved, father and son became more aware of the familiar music of the countryside. Tugging on his father's arm, the son quickly led the way to the souvenir of their enchanted passing. As he respectfully held the shining feather, remembrance of its delivery kissed their minds. They walked homewards, knowing their bodies would not obey a day's hard work, under a mind that cared only to replay a moment of enchanted splendour.

Later, when the sky exchanged her cloak, they sat by the

farmhouse fire, exhausted by their enthusiastic telling of the tale to the mother, which had left room for her wisdom to settle, and the fire to lick away unheard words of secrets. Then, as quick as intuition came to her, the woman brought a sharp knife to her husband and mimed her wish. He took the sharpness to the feather, and by the act of playfully waving it over some paper annouced the feather, a fine golden quill.

The quick hand of youth took hold and claimed it as his own. Bidding his parents goodnight, he laid down his excited head to dream. His dreaming went wandering, turning right, then right again, not knowing where it was leading, yet following the misty steps of an entwining staircase and climbing onwards, even as they became narrow and hidden. He doubted his steadfastness and questioned his sense, but the light of his reason shone before him, encouraging him on. Just then, his eyes became heavy and then closed, by a will outside his own. He made no attempt to oppose it, as a knowing told his mood of melancholy that this sleepwalk would soon awake to a vision of euphoria. An air of change shifted around his dream skin, yet he questioned not his new cloak of manliness, just as the chrysalis accepts gifts of

3

flight and colour.

Then, like candle glow born from the darkness, came a garden scene of rhapsody. Obeying the desire still, he walked on through invisible waves of empathy and clemency. Gazing around, he discovered a beautiful land, truly refined in colour and form. Nature's exceptional goodness lay courteous all around, bestowing her elegance to all as she lay in quiet repose. Stopping to smell the very rose that demented a poet for a most earnest phrase, he heard the tumbling laughter of a fountain share its jolly silver children with a red sun. An emerald lawn laid a passing melody of pardons about his toes, then beckoned him deeper into the journey.

His mind finally reached a mantle, as he sensed a living light growing from behind him, enveloping his space. Shifting his focus, his gaze fell mindful into a most beautiful pair of ice-blue eyes. Just as a feather succumbs to a palm, his consciousness floated deeper into the bejewelled eyes.

The good soldier crumbled to his knees, unable to bear the love from this most spiritual of lights. Then this great core of reality bequeathed a truth, and spoke the good soldier's spiritual name. At once, his mind drifted even higher, into a tender embrace of this great mother, yet also father, who showered utter devotion upon him. Here, embraced in the bosom of eternity, warm and understood, he lay in close company with many other children, who had also journeyed to the heart of their spiritual home.

Snuggled together in unlimited love, the great light of everything whispered truths to all those children embraced: the dew of the lotus; the hurt that forgave; the child that existed as a memory; the reward for a virtue returned; the minute of one's own need surrendered to tend to another's hour, full of want. Plus many more of one and the same, hearing the flow of cream making notes of music upon the tongue of the good creator, as great love voiced its claim, singing:

"I have divided myself into many parts. You are of me and I of you. Feel unconnected no more, my children, for you are with the greatest part of you, which art in heaven. An angel left the door of heaven ajar; your light slipped through and found thy kingdom. Your desire saddled your free will, riding your will on earth, as it is in heaven. Be empty no more. I am the daily bread, the feast for spiritual hunger. Many trespasses you have dined and lain with, against your brother. Forgiveness is a barefoot road, with many stones. The light is of you, born from the death of temptation, worn as the cloak of deliverance from all evil. Love me and live me, by my name - love unconditional; know there is no other kingdom. I am the power and the glory of that name. From this day forward, accept that I am the master of your soul, for ever and ever."

The piercing blue eyes of kindness lowered with the greatest of humility, then released a question to the good soldier's awareness, prompting his reply.

"To be with my spirit is to be with the light of you. To experience a silent mind is to be with the peace of you. To serve compassionately is to feed the heart of you. To know your laws is to be guided by you."

Unconditional love birthed a tear through the eye of compassion, a reward for the living of God's love. The good soldier's gratitude collected it and pinned it to his heart. Then, again, great liberation spoke.

"It is by no light thought that you are guardian of the quill, so let it be that the words from the golden quill shall crown laws of truth on the minds of my children and cloak their spirits with the cloth of their testimony. Return to the world of simple reflection and live the plan, knowing that you suckle milk and honey from the bosom of eternity with each breath until I call you again."

A mist engulfed him, rendered his mind numb, then spiralled his awareness downwards towards his physical body. Countryside sounds aroused his sleepy senses homewards, waking to his mother's elated welcome, and his father's consolable frown told him that he had lived away longer than any dream. His physique mirrored the feasting of milk and honey whilst in the true kingdom.

From this very day of his awakening, he penned a university of the Lord's love for the education of the villagers. Guided well by the laws, aware that encouragement can be the birth of inspiration and criticism its death, he served well.

One day he spoke to those who learn through grace. "As all streams run to one sea, you, my children, have travelled like the crystal waters that wear a cold, silvery cloak of deception. Your emotions cloaked your spirit so well that your trust fell into the well of despair, when all the while your soul was able. When your ignorance drowned your reasoning, judgement fell against the rocks at the foot of the waterfall, bashed and shattered,

7

sinking into every corner of self. But the current of life's experiences collected you and reunited your strengths to your same good self, leaving you supple and clear enough to accept your differences."

One day he spoke to those who learn from humility. "Crop of children that experience being rooted on this earth, let the heat of life's hardships fertilise and ripen your humility. Accept that its lessons can be the break from the husk of karma. When the raping season comes, know that it is merely a death of the chaff. All goodness from the crop is baled and only hard seeds are sown again, to rebirth towards a soul-refining grain that one day will be served as our father's daily bread, feeding all who hunger, discriminating against none."

One day he spoke to those who learn from liberty. "If you can truly say that you kept your bird of liberty content within its cage, that it never squawked or flapped in frustration to live the free expression through its wings, even when the other birds pecked and rattled their cage with wings of flaming hot temper, then maybe, just maybe, you know liberty. But if you never once cried for those birds, for the loss of their freedom to be that true expressive thing with wings, then maybe, just maybe, you only ever perched yourself on the bar of indifference."

One day he spoke to those who learn from nobleness. "To serve unconditionally is noble. Simply as a great ship, which sets sail on many seas, in any storm; a carrier who accepts all cargo."

Many moons and suns had passed when the day came for change. The clouds bounced about the horizon and the air was filled with balloons of talk from the villagers busy in the market square, who were totally unaware of the awesome wonder that was to collect the teenager of manly mind and manners; the young servant, who had sat amongst them, sharing the way of the great, good heart.

As if the stars fell into day, the villagers gasped in awesome wonder, As first they witnessed a pair of giant claws land sharp and quick, swiftly followed by the full impact of God's goodwill on wings. The good soldier greeted his ally and then, gripping tightly onto the stole of stable feathers, he hoisted himself onto the back of the golden phoenix, slid his slender legs behind its massive wings, then sank up to his waist in a cascade of plumage. As he turned to see his parents empty of his touch, an invisible ghost of truth patted his shoulder, with the comfort that they would witness his safe departure. The

9

slow, soft nod of his head was all his father needed to accept that his child went as a man who knew his task. Then, for his mother, he shed one solitary tear, the very last left from his childhood.

Their departure was swift and sure, leaving the villagers with quiet, open expressions. After silence had lived for some while, his parents standing trapped in a non-verbal, mournful gaze, suddenly their eyes found comfort in familiarity, as floating downwards from the sky came a black felt hat. As they clasped onto the hat for joy, a shaft of light pierced through, for tight in the rim was a tiny gift for his mother, immortalised in crystal - his tear.

Mystical wings offloaded its precious cargo, unchaperoned, high up on a mountain, then swiftly took flight, leaving him dizzy from dancing with the twisted sisters - curiosity and dreaming. His feet tested the rocky pathway, as winds bashed about him. A few more steps uncovered a ragged cave, for sanctuary. Falling into this quiet, still space, he laid down his tired bones, teasing the floor beneath him in an effort to find comfort. He gazed out the cave to the scene below, across acres of forest and waterfalls. His here and now spoke to him of cold and thirst. As he wrapped his empty arms around him as a lowly blanket, a salty drop of anticipation broke free from its promise of strength. Just then, birds listened and winds held their breath, for they recognised the arrival of Omell, the angel of sleep, who in her very presence had the fragrance of ether. Her goodnight kiss bade farewell to his yesterdays, and out of her invisibleness came a blanket of darkness, to cover mortal bones until, or if, its owner resided again.

In his sleep, a misty lady of silver thread spun quick from his breath, drawing out stale aching wants that died a death by spoken fears and idle reason; clearing through every empty opinion and blind ignorance, in a time before the plan was told; pouring every drop of his today through the well of time. Ending the journey of the good soldier, so another could begin.

THE GOOD SCHOLAR

Reaching taller than any dream and wider than any dimension stood the great wall of spent eternity - the vault of entire history, of moments lived, entered as scrolls, books, deeds or thoughts. Wiping the sleep from his eyes, the entirety of it all engulfed the good scholar's acceptance, yet shone little light of reason. He cried out, "I make no claim to dream such a colossal carousel of moments, yet I question this reality, why it fills my nostrils sweet and of a heavy garment of flesh, I am free?"

His heart beat fast with creeping intrigue at the sensing of many breaths, lived in deed or thought. Then, gently reaching to touch the prize of life, barely for the briefest moment, his ethereal fingers touched God's greatest gift to man - free will. Yet each passing event crested over him like the breaking of a wave, saturating his senses, ebbing murmurs of empathy from his lips. The scholar's mild manner touched many things, in shame and honour, as man's deeds bed down for eternal sleep, for evermore to mark their time, embalmed in the name of excellence, or sacrilege.

Experiences raced through every one of his senses, the partition of daggers soiled with blood ink: the bladed pens, by which many countrymen signed their signature, in the back of mad Caesar; tears of applause that wept from amphitheatres, as the Grecian performers circled tissues of acoustics to dry their appreciation; white tears of women, bound by a ming dynasty, that long to unbind their disciplined steps. He touched life's great tapestry, seeing the unique stitch of eureka, sewn by the thread of one man's achievements, and felt the anger that guillotined a revolution, bringing the reign of aristocrats and the dogged poor pouring into Parisian streets.

Still the good scholar glided forward, learning as he went of each man's reason and search for truth. All the while, he mumbled God's teaching, applying the spiritual dressing to the open wounds of faulty humanity. He saw, too, that no great ruler came to be by measuring his intelligence and abilities by that of another. Six million signatures penned in blood and terror, for not an Arian race is born. The new children of King David have had this promise sworn. He felt the splash as the giant, shy man of the moon kind jumped into the Sea of Tranquillity, as the small foot of bold kind claimed it giant. He felt all the people cry as one, as a bullet shot the dreamer, although he imaged that he's not the only one. He saw the monster of commerce dance and sing to meet its agent, the media. He saw how one man created a band of aid to wrap around the starving world, feeding many bellies and souls with notes of awareness.

He spied ahead for a moment, to view the end was near. Only words that were to be written lay by books with pages bare. Miles of existence had he acknowledged in the speeding of his flight to arrive at the tip of life's bookcase and a twinkling pair of eyes and a voice that spoke. "Only those that live to my rhythm could know the tears of my children, and accept why I do not take away their pain."

And the good scholar replied, "You make no claim of their strength to overcome the hardest of lessons - to be in this world, yet not of this world."

Seeing the good creator pleased, he sighed; his task was now surely done. But little did the scholar realise that the plan had only just begun. The melting phrase of poetry spelt his plan to the good scholar:

"True wisdom has just been born. See before you an empty scroll. Spill upon it realisations of your journey. See, too, a fine golden quill. The feather that you knew before was merely a replica of its shadowy twin."

Once again the good scholar became of service, searching every part of himself that could experience. Then he set sail on a boat of salvation upon the harrowing waves of life's hard sea, to share with others that all spirits can sail homeward if they navigate around the rocks of reality.

Writing, man should see the privilege in doing a duty. If that duty is of spiritual service, then the privilege is in the earning of that duty. The ego builds a staircase that the soul shall never climb. Controlling your thoughts houses peace of mind and neighbouring tranquillity to live with others. If self-control is willpower and right thought is mastery, then calmness within is peace of mind and love is harmony. All sensitivity has to be mastered before it can be of any aim, or else it just wanders in a mist of emotional targets. It's mostly the lazy underachiever that is quick to assume that there's no task in learning the skill that someone has mastered. Yet the student that has mastered the aptitude to learn has achieved the formula for learning. Seek not outward applause from others, but rather the inward, contented compliment of one's own mind. Why have people always worried about death when they constantly kill their spirit by the slaying hand of self-doubt? A man should never compromise his virtues, because he foresees the consequences. It's the spirit inside that should do the striding and the body the abiding, not the other way round.

Unrequested, a silver throne smothered with cherubs appeared to rest his swollen heart, weak from spent humility. Upon seeing this, he fell to his knees with his hands clasped in devotional prayers. A new breeze blew in from somewhere else and brushed little pink kisses upon his skin, melting into his soul and creating a space for him to dream melodiously - that to share would be to dilute.

THE GOOD MASTER

At the cool waters of the stream, the still reflection of truth was broken with thirsty glad tidings. His soul and body were now aged with insight and the sleep of a thousand dreams, existing as a phantom of reality and a witness to great change.

A bird on high rang out its poisoned cry of sorrow, which twined with his rare, lonesome thought of self. Suddenly a lyrical wind blew, and he captured its psalm with a tear - his last salty drop of misunderstanding. His cold bones called for warmth and, as trust always creates, wood and an axe appeared beside him.

After time had passed, warm and calm, he put out the fire and hid the axe behind a huge boulder. Then the spirit liberty took his hand and called him by his spirit name, the good master, and bade him to walk his fragile bones towards the distant soup of civilisation. As the path opened before him, he beheld a tureen of minds and manners at market. It seemed all had brought their crafts and produce. The good master perched his bony body, then waited with spiritual appetite. His first course of humanity stood before him: a woman with quick intuition and her five sons. Hustling their heads with ugly farmhouse hands, she manoeuvred them in order of height, as if to prepare them for his inspection. They giggled in shy anticipation of his approval, as he made play on his face to humour any impatience of his elderly shuffling pace towards them.

With a quiet sigh and great compassion, he greeted her maternal eyes displaying a pleading stare, as she said, "Truly you are the walking scriptures. Bestow truths to my young sons' minds."

He lowered his eyes with his greatest humility and replied, "I will give to your children as our lord gives to his children. I shall give them that which they need, that they may be healed. I shall give them that which they want, that they may learn by it."

The first son was a child of the water, who owned a purposeful will, plus a great appreciation of the emotions. With him the good master shared, "Grace is within you, and by this you may learn simply how to be."

Then, inspired further, he added, "Accept all waves of

emotions. Let them flow to and fro with equality. Question not the reality of that wave, but that of your dreams they leave behind, for they are the true emotion of change. After that wave has lived, be still, be centred, be aware, and be now.

"The light of men has given everyone just a little bit more than they thought they could handle. Simply reach and grasp to find the cure of your torment.

"Empty your pain by my sea, and bring your silver children to me. Hurt and you stand alone, bearing soul, on pebble honeycomb. As emotional knots unravel, not hide, swim out to full moon and tide. Tears stream to earth's well, talking faulty humanity in ear of shell. Swim silver children, by light of the moon, not freed from a promise too soon,"

With this, the child of water ran off to fetch some wine for the good master's expectant thirst.

The second son was a child of the fire, who owned goodwill, plus a great appreciation of the mental. With him the good master shared, "Nobleness is within you, and by this you may learn simply how to serve."

Then, inspired further, he added, "Wealthy is the man who finds a quality within, nurtures it, then gives it away to others.

"Thoughts of yesterday lie easy, like moss on a rock in a stagnant pond. Thoughts of tomorrow rise and froth with muddy expectations. Where is the still clean water that the spirit will drink today?

"All that is ever required is clear, correct, communication. Conclusions are delivered and answers are developed. Always and forever aim to possess a clear mind, a clear heart and a clear path.

"Develop a motive for each action. Beforehand is wise; after is a learning."

With this the child of the fire ran off to fetch a book for the good master's expectant tired reason.

The third son was a child of the air, who owned unconditional will, plus a great appreciation of the spirit. With him the good master shared, "Liberty is within you, and by this you may learn simply how to know."

Then, inspired further, he added, "Confidence resides within the heart that speaks words of truth, whether spoken to one ear or many, and the message of goodness is the same.

"The words from the fruitful spirit are ripe. Each word is sown from the seed of truth. Each word is grown from the seed of truth.

"It is said that a man of great wisdom, never steps upon the earth, but walks upon the stones of realisation, just above.

"As our creator's quiet eyes watch us, he can see the ego burn the white flag of goodwill, clip the wings of the dove of liberty, get drunk on the wine of emotions and tear down trees by want and willpower."

With this, the child of the air ran off to fetch some cloth for the good master's expectant chill.

The fourth son was a child of the earth, who owned willpower, plus a great appreciation of the physical. With him the good master shared, "Humility is within you, and by this you may learn simply how to experience."

Then, inspired further, he added, "When the walk of your here and now slips down the well of daydreams, make watch your busy hands at daily chores. Have your thoughts walk in the light of the mind.

"Change is not born by a maternal push and shove, but by the courteous appreciation of development, as all natural growth springs unexpected.

"Your spirit is clothed in the heavy cloth of skin to walk this school of unlimited learning. Remember neither spirit

21

nor flesh is ever what it is, but rather what it can become."

With this, the child of the earth ran off to fetch some bread, for the good master's expectant hunger.

The fifth son was a child of the moon, sun and stars, who owned no will of his own, but simply lived the will of the creator, plus a great love of all. With him the good master shared, "For you are a true merit of the elements, and your will shall simply come to know the experience of being of service to the divine."

Then, inspired further, he added, "Little spirituality comes from philosophy; it is simply mental. Little spirituality comes from tears; it is simply emotion. Little spirituality comes from fasting; it is simply physical. Big spirituality comes from prayer; it is simply spiritual.

"In one single breath you are in the quiet company of the divine. Breathe in, accept divine. Hold breath, surrender divine. Breathe out, release divine."

The fifth son's feet stood quiet and still, so the good master asked, "Why do you not expect and run to fetch?

The boy replied, "The entire world presumes it, when really it should all depend. Then, just when they accept the probable, they go and suppose over again."

Gradually a mumbling crowd gathered around the good

master, as food fit for a king and fine woven cloth were laid out before him. Seeing the bountiful spread, he raised his eyes to the fifth son and said, "I am too weak to partake of this feast, or dress so fair in grace. But now, as my spirit leaves me, I shall know them in a more heavenly place."

Now in silence the crowd looked on and prayed for his spirit's safe journey. Far off in the distance, a bird's cry could be heard. The last son cleared his mind, cleared his heart, then saw before him a clear path, and on that path he heard his name - his true spiritual name.

VIRTUE OF THE ELEMENTS

WATER

His perfect frame of bones sighed, surrendering the small of his back to the palm of the earth. His curls spiralled and bounced golden, on a beautiful brain that ate life's daily bread, smothered with the sauce of childish wonder. A warm afternoon breeze, whose only luggage was the joys of summer and the occasional dry, creaking moan from the sycamore tree that circled overhead, meant little more than grumpy nonsense to the youthful mind underneath contemplating play. Mother Nature cradled him in her warm cleavage like a babe, his physicalness suckled to the ground. His long lashes swept away the sky's unreachable jigsaw, opening in slow motion to a beam of diamond dust. The cherub youth, named Jeremiah, made it shrink then enlarge, as he filtered the sunlight through the slits of his eyelids.

As he rested his mind on nothing in particular, Jeremiah's hearing stumbled upon a constant, distant piercing. This poor man's peace claimed itself important by its boastful shrilling. His concentration boarded the coach of appreciation, as he discovered its apparent singing of high pitches and higher still. His eyesight unemployed of any mindful attention brought his mind to focus on the level of their dry stare. With this he realised that he had discovered a small twitching world, where pale microscopic worms danced in a sunbeam. As he watched in amazed concentration, he felt a subtle shifting of his brain, as right and left hemispheres cleaved firmly together, discovering alpha. Time and space became a single moment that he occupied with a subtle knowing that he was nearly gone.

One of the wriggling species halted its apparent nonsense of writhing and began to pulse with illumination. Jeremiah understood that this was recognition of his presence and a message of welcome. His strong, inquisitive desire to explore made every improbability possible. A vacuum inside his forehead grew in turbulence, formed a tunnel, then gathered all his desire to experience into its pink furry comfort.

From the glove of the material world, he landed with a bump into a world that shared a secret of volume, because beneath his chubby, bare feet were massive, rounded pebbles. Handsome in colour were the true-blue sapphires, sunset-orange topaz and Irish-meadow emeralds. Taking a kind hold without intrusion, he bent down and cupped a crisp emerald. His excitement ate wonder as he touched its solidness, then completely feasted when he realised that he held a mere grain of sand, and had entered a land where jewels were as free as sand; meaning that surely if these gifts had not been plundered, any entity he encountered would be without lust for profit.

With this knowing, his confidence crept out of its shell to walk the short distance to the water's edge. He proceeded without fear into the beckoning blue waves, crumbling like small walls as he waded deeper. Cobalt blue met his chin, and still fear never showed its face. A serene calmness had been born unto his understanding when he first came to be in this land and remained strong, even now as the chilly depth came to the top of his fair head. As he let out the last precious air from his lungs, new breath became liquid, running chilly down his throat. Three times he drank away the breath of the sea, and with each he felt his legs mat together like the tail of a fish.

Floating comfortably in stillness and half form, a rhythmic lullaby cradled Jeremiah, rocking him to peace. An inner knowing told his soul to succumb while obedience slid him deep into a wash of meditation, totally transforming him and now wearing the cloth of an enormous golden fish. His joy bowed with applause at being able to explore this path safely, wearing the expression of fish.

Movement came like a natural course of action as his scales bent and twisted, slithering through the fluent reflection of the skies. Passing before him came a feminine shell creature, pieced together like patchwork. Her language of motion was of beguiling poetry. She paddled through the abyss, breaking the veil before her and leaving the sea sorrowful in her passing; crying bubble tears to the surface, breaking through the rippling undercurrent that flexed its masculinity, as if it were the taut belly of Atlas.

Spying a dark rock ahead, curiosity flapped his tail faster. Moving closer still, he figured it to be a huge snake, twisting and writhing, as if to undo its knotted self. Closer still, he could see that it was a tornado of tiny fish, swimming with perfect synchronisation yet shaped by

27

fear. Playfulness ran to Jeremiah's fins, urging him to dive into their fear disguise. With lightness in his heart to change their false proclamation of bravery, he swam towards them.

Suddenly a dark apparition fell from out of the cold, barging into the scene, with grey rubber skin and white needle-sharp teeth. Its hard quickness cut up silver pearls of play that had just passed Jeremiah a moment ago, before throwing them away with one calculating bash of its forked tail. The thrashing double-edged sword came slashing and diving towards the untrue form of snake. Driven by the angry eye of hunger, its gnashers chased down the back of those uniformed in fear. Jeremiah's eyes widened in shocked, hot temper, boiling the water around him, sharpening each and every golden scale he wore. A steaming tornado bullet of energy shot fierce before him, charging like a bull aimed true and straight. Its delivery wrapped tight around its belly, landing taut spasms of burning shock, defusing that most explosive shark dynamite.

Freed from its jaws, the fish flew swift away with their scaly wings, tailing behind Jeremiah to a safe place of warm, still blue. Jeremiah's golden armour relaxed with relief and peace at the change of their flow behind him. He turned, expecting to see them unite into their uniform of snake. Instead he saw a replica of himself, crafted from hundreds of tiny fish, riding in the wake of his powerful wash. His heart gave flight, as though born with wings, as an understanding filled his knowing that another blueprint of evolution had been created.

As the sunlight rode through the sea, the fish circled Jeremiah, dressing him in their close swim. Jeremiah's stare fell into the shine of their metallic, shimmering armour. Within this slithering mercury he saw a large fish, with jewelled vibrancy and long, elegant fins that trailed and twitched with each watery ripple. Into this silent watchfulness his hearing woke to a singing, ringing sound. Taking on a fish's natural characteristics, he looked into the noise by feeling its vibrations. The obvious sprang to his mind. This music had been a constant, distant companion that he had often heard drifting in the background, but now, as he listened attentively, he understood it to be compiled from the sounds of elements and composed by the sea wind. Wafting from the blueness, the sea wind played the flowing locks of fishy maidens like a soulful harp, the haunting gallop of seahorses, the clapping of delighted clams, and the tears of homesick seamen shattering on the surface. The deeper he focused, the clearer the music became. Little by little, his hearing opened to hear someone talking musically.

Just then a voice with controlled syllables circled his name around him, "Je- re - mi - ah." His fishy body became clumsy and twitched as he felt his personal space shrink. Softly the voice said, "The reflection in the living mercury is a part of your spirit, which is akin to the waters. A time comes to each spirit when they are blessed to go and collect a reward fitting to his virtue and spiritual growth. Jeremiah, your time has come. Go into the realm of virtues and think of positive, justly rewards."

These words of wisdom covered his reasoning like thick, good butter on homemade bread. Jeremiah closed his eyes, stilled his sharp golden tail, then opened his young mind, to a land where all is fair. His mouth gulped, involuntary to fishy ways, creating a big, wobbly bubble.

Melting 24-carat-gold sang instructions. "Think yourself into that bubble, young friend."

Inch by inch, he disappeared. When his wagging tail was the last to be seen, the bubble popped into small, stiff air pockets, leaving only his colourful twin basking in the sun, sharing the best-kept secret of the deep. For, as the high sun reflected upon beautiful scales, a beam shot up through the water, becoming an arched garland in the sky, showing his beauty in the air, and his pot of gold to all.

Jeremiah slipped from one circle of consciousness to another; his transport, the strong back of his willpower, and his map, a faithful desire to fulfil his quest for rewards. Jeremiah swam through seven circles, which barely seemed linked but were held together strong and secure by the thumb and forefinger of the highest will. In these links was a short space without time. He collected his reward and sparks of knowledge from a creative link that man discovers when he uses the key of imagination, slides through the gap of déjà vu, or rests his mind on nothing in particular.

All too soon, Jeremiah heard the song, "Share the story of your rewards, Jeremiah."

Jeremiah sat in a space abundant with light, and then shared the story of his reward. "I was in my spiritual home, and one morning woke early, so set about my daily chores. I thought to fetch some water from the well, so disturbed my quiet pail from its corner. I stepped out onto crystallised grass, and became aware that I was in a time before dawn. Nature lay sleeping all about and in the haze of the moonlight; daisies stood closed, yet on parade, each like a bundle of tiny quills. My mind felt the subtle presence of Mother Moon, attentively watching over Sister Earth. Her misty silver cloak caught my mind in an azure dream and faintly she showed me that her sleep had nearly come, paying appreciation to a sweet posy of twilight, a lilac tree and newly barbered grass, which rose up from juicy, thawing dew. I was in kind company of watchful eyes and harmony rising. My feet continued the journey to labour the well of its pearly children, who carry the cross of all tears.

"In the dripping echo of this long pool, my perspective fell through the aperture of darkness, making my concentration a meditation. I gathered my pail filled with deep mirror into capable hands of balance. The borrowed water reformed with ease upon the splashing of my taut walk, and from the pail I could hear its pearls of merry laughter.

"Returning towards my cottage, I saw Father Sun create a brand new day, as he peeled the blanket of earth away from him. His majesty was my privilege, although it was he who bowed to me, inviting me to eat the sweet bread of that new day. My breakfast was the talk of the trees as they warmed, yawning and stretching, reaching their gnarled arms with many elbows towards a different air, which rang with early morning prayers from tiny, plumed souls that sang away the sleep in their small black eyes.

"Just then, I came upon a pure golden beam of sunlight that rode a path from my toes to my little wooden door. In that path were the daisies, awake with all the privileges of light, some still opening as if tiny suns being born before me. My good heart whispered to me of humility, so I took away my wear of shoes. This blessed path of nobleness felt like pink kisses on my souls, and humbleness cherished their flowery invitation to make my journey homeward a favour of honour.

"Walking by the twinned light of my garden guardians, compassion cupped my steps fragile upon the fallen suns. Then I heard a robin redbreast sing, like a medal for my soul. When I reached my little wooden door, I found his song had named it and pinned it to my heart. And written on it was my virtue and my soul's reward of grace."

FIRE

Jeremiah's eyes opened wide to a structure of high wooden arches, empty in ease and ignorant of daylight. All above him heaved and bowed with massive wooden ribs. He gazed downwards to a long, narrow, arched opening with a thick, cold stone lip that yawned a sigh of light. Beyond this gaping, toothless mouth, Jeremiah could see a small walled garden laden with flowers. A crude seat rested near a dark oak door, with black iron bolts and studs. Sitting quite contrary on the farthest, darkest corner was a small grey stone table. Upon it he could see a book, leather bound, with embossed spine and fine edges of gold, all cherished securely with filigree clasps.

Bringing his awareness still and inwards, Jeremiah could sense his energy was enclosed within a small square cove. From nowhere a yawn came from his belly, which became a hard bellow that shot forward like a rod tongue. On its return he felt a coolness melting like a taste of saviour, and he understood at once that the sooty blackness was his former skin, the yawn his hunger and the coolness his daily bread. He set out to enjoy himself a little, popping and cracking in the air, shooting sparks across the hall, then eating some more to grow.

Just then, the door creaked, intruding on his fun. Pushing through was a young girl, whose steps were short and quick as she carried a full pail of water. She sat the pail tight in a shadowy corner, tidied her long dress about her neatly, rolled her sleeves to her elbows, and then started to clean the stone floor. She moved across the floor, wetting it shiny to the ugly music of the scrubbing brush. The echoes of the rhythmic circles entranced Jeremiah, as they piled on top of one another.

When daylight bowed to an evening moon, she stood as empty as her pail. Aching and hunched from bending, she made her way towards the beautiful book. But it was too late. No light came through the window for her to read by. She reluctantly replaced the book and closed the door behind her.

For the next five days, the same picture of refined self-discipline, laborious chore and sad consequence came before Jeremiah, who felt no presence of the song and lived confused and frustrated at what he had witnessed. Yet not once did she moan or frown in her obvious misery. On the sixth day Jeremiah, still unsure of his role in all this, could hold his desire to help this soul no longer. By his very will to help, a part of himself in the form of fire flew into her bucket. The water hissed as it turned from icy cold to luke warm. He swam for a while, making sure of its change. Thinking himself into the chilly air around her, he left the bucket and became warmth.

Feeling the difference of the water from the day before, the young girl looked out to the piece of sky through the long arched window and said, "For I am truly blessed." She enthusiastically splashed her hand into the pail and sped her way through the arduous task. The faster she scrubbed, the quicker Jeremiah danced around her, faster and faster to the rhythm of her work, drying the floor behind her. Upon noticing a pleasant difference in the air, she raised her head, looked out to the sky and again said, "For I am truly blessed."

This time her tedious chore was completed well in advance. She leapt to her feet, dried her hands in the warm air, dashed across the hall to the awaiting book and, granted by the light of the sun, began to read.

Jeremiah felt the coals of contentment burn deep within him. In this stillness he could hear bells ringing. His fire opened up with a happy roar, as he knew it to be the singing voice. "Je-re-mi-ah, fall into the cradle of sleep. Do this and you will be free to return to the garden of virtue."

Jeremiah did the bidding of the song and found himself in the garden. The air waved currents of fragrant kisses to his cheek as a welcome. Just then, Jeremiah heard his name spoken; subtle enough, as though he had overheard a conversation. He waited silently, daring it to be repeated. Shortly, he heard his name mentioned again. He fluted back a note of question. "Excuse me, are you talking to me?"

With this, a voice with the clarity of perfume called out. "Jeremiah, look for me!"

Characters - unquestionable obedience and curiosity - became companions, leading him forward a few steps. But he saw nothing.

The high voice called out once again. "Look for me, Jeremiah!"

Thinking himself clever this time, he nosed down to the shrubs, matching the tiny voice with an obvious small hiding place. As he roamed on his hands and knees, Nature's chiffon softly touched his face, bringing a passion of that very bloom to his lips with an uncontrolled sigh, which travelled down the funnel of velvet, devouring his salute as a meal. Immediately he mislaid his quest, as his stare became dry and lost in its ease of beauty.

This calm awareness collected his mind higher, opening his senses to a florid language. For the flowers were in talk, sharing with the summer wind their secrets. Their subtle meanings filled up and over petals, dripping them lovely into a teeny leaved basket, as though an emotional balm soothing a misunderstanding. A tiny, chubby hand with baby-pink skin had this duty tied pretty with a bow.

Brown eyes, as round and shiny as buttons, dived their glare into the gazing pools of Jeremiah's. Every inch a fairy, she stood plump and cute, dressed in bluebell silk and wild poppy ribbon. Sunlight bounced about her crown of hazelnut hair and shimmered on her dainty petalled wings. Her wide eyes sparkled when she spoke. "More would look, if only they knew me true. But the few who look unknowing find what many never do."

Afraid of losing this vision of floral wonder to a hope

fulfilled by his imagination, Jeremiah slowly shook his head from side to side, viewing her from each corner of his eyes, to see if she was true. The fairy slowly did the same, ending her cheeky mimic with a shy chuckle that tickled the roses beside her, as they looked on in melting admiration.

She pointed a fine finger, preparing him for a statement. "Your wish is to give a posy, expressing the love in your heart. Just choose the flowers by their talk and your words the bouquet will impart."

His hands rose up in prayer to his smiling lips, a totally unaware display of his delight at her charm and assumption of his visit. For he had not, until meeting this blessing, had any inclination as to the reason for his visit.

Jeremiah's voice softened considerably, afflicted by her cuteness. "Dear winged soul, please tell me who you are and what you do."

Her bluebell dress curled up as she sat down on a leaf. She then placed the basket of precious nectar close beside her and poetically proclaimed, "They say a little kindness goes a long way. But did you know a flower grows with each kind word you say. The seeds they are a selfless gesture or a silent compliment; the healing hand of care, to souls hurt with life's ailments. A truly sincere charity smells of a more powerful perfume, and a soul such as this always finds his garden in bloom. I'm Scentina, born from human kindness. That is why I'm not very tall. There's precious little of it, but I have the nicest parents of all."

With this, Jeremiah lost a tear he had been saving for later. Scentina immediately picked up her basket and flew up to the trickle on his cheek. She flapped her iridescent wings near to his face and said, "Not one drop of kindness goes to waste." She gazed into the basket with love filling her eyes. "That drop of kindness is for me, I think, from my father Jeremiah."

With such a big understanding from such a tiny soul, a few more drops of kindness appeared for her basket, and she collected them just the same, ordering, "Now go about your business, or else you'll wash away." With this, she buzzed her wings, kissed him tenderly on the nose and flew high up and over a magnolia.

Jeremiah stood up, dried his eyes and then set about picking a bouquet for his overworked, silent companion. The language of flowers sang out like a choir in the

40

midday heat, explaining away their names with musical pleasure. The honeysuckle sang of sweet disposition, whilst the laurel-leaved magnolia tuned to a song of dignity. Snowdrops harmonised ever hopeful, as a lone star of Bethlehem whispered a carol of purity. Lily of the valley echoed a good return of happiness, comforting the purple lilac, which cried over the first emotions of love. A two-toned pansy reached high notes of good thoughts, under a strong oak who boosted a tenor of bravery. The proud mulberry tree gave away words of generosity whilst its flowers hummed along with charity. But the roses sang the sweetest. Rose monteflora sang softly of grace whilst the great crown rose was soprano, singing always a reward for a virtue.

Jeremiah strolled along a winding path lined with a menu of benevolence. He dined deliciously on a floral banquet of delicate phrases, choosing pure delights from Nature's kitchen. The thick honeyed air soon rendered Jeremiah dreamy, as a fuchsia bade him snooze under the great oak, declaring his choice was complete and in the finest of taste. Shade brought meditation creeping into his sleep, shaping his spirit beautiful into the dance of the butterfly.

With this transformation done, he awoke to the sounds of happiness flying from his heart. "I am the ever breath." Jeremiah smelt his sweet body and realised that he held the fragrance of the flowers within him. "I'll return to my friend with their perfume about me," he said cheerfully.

As always, the thought was the deed. He glided around the building, became a draught, and then squeezed through the gap in the window. There sat the young girl, reading by the grace of afternoon sunlight. Becoming aware of the change in air, she closed her eyes to her book and began slowly to inhale the new air. Jeremiah hung captured in complete stillness. For before him, he witnessed a silvery mist emanating from within her, swirling around her heart in a circle, faster and faster. Particles of silver mist thickened and began to manifest through the haze. Finally the mist cleared, leaving a solid silver rose.

Jeremiah sucked inwards, whirling a token of perfume. He softly released his perfume near the heart of the magical rose. With this, a movement like soft, shifting sands came upon the petals, which unfurled gracefully to the fragrance. Deep within its heart, Jeremiah could see a pearl of golden nectar, and in it a reflection of a tiny, chubby hand. A silent compliment opened the young girl's eyes slowly. She gazed straight into the space that was Jeremiah, releasing an echo from a heart that had received. "For I am truly blessed."

AIR

Jeremiah's curiosity questioned what was next on the agenda of spiritual discovery and the meaning of air, with its continual folding and unfolding. The youth knew to explore for spiritual growth, although he longed to scratch the itch to play, so he screamed about in an excited rush, falling into giggles as his easy body tumbled and turned into itself. In so doing, he discovered that air has no passing, simply a changing of substance that has the power to turn a harmless, lazy sigh into a monster whirlwind.

The earth looked snug under a huge, sprouting quilt. He knew she lay not asleep, but was working quietly and constantly, pulsing the major veins of earth life, with a heart that is the disciplined warp and the body the shifting weft; constantly weaving a beautiful tapestry with yarns that ebb and flow and sow and reap, all made beautiful by the great weaver.

Jeremiah noticed lines upon lines of far-reaching wire,

and balanced upon these were small, winged fancies. Some sat clustered and others singly, but together looked like the notes of a tune. Wondering what music their presence would make, Jeremiah brought forward a back part of himself and howled through, plucking them with his near ethereal fingers. Their tune he knew well. It grew clearer as towards him the anthem sang, "Je-re-mi-ah!"

In a panic of joy, he answered, "Yes, I'm here. See me, and hear me."

His only constant companion tuned back, "Hel-loo dancing Je-re-mi-ah."

To this playful tune, Jeremiah in pleasure rushed around in all directions.

"Je-re-mi-ah!"

Jeremiah stopped still in his tracks, ready to hear what was often little, but important news.

"Your task you will uncover in time. Playing upon the land you already know how to do. I have been watching your play. Journey and discover."

With the last of these words the song vanished, leaving Jeremiah standing quietly alone in a corner of himself. Suddenly, behind the door of opportunity, a draught of sadness blew through. Within it, he felt the tight belt of human awareness, pulled taut by punishing ego. Upon this realisation, he knew his play was over.

Over the next few days, Jeremiah worked hard, cleaning and sweeping like a maid, air doing the housework of the land. He likened his body to an enormous flapping overcoat with many gaping pockets. Some collected debris, such as negative thoughts and feelings. Others, charged with precious inspiration, sprinkled little but often, their load falling as freely as raindrops and yet taken for granted just the same. Jeremiah worked hard until he had carved stone, sailed boats, carried prayers, upheld wings, inspired artists, sowed seeds and dried tears the best he could.

Then, one day, while Jeremiah was by the waters of St Justin Roseland, he heard a soft whisper. "Many vibrations you hold as the medium between heaven and earth. Find a voice to sing your messages for that is air's true gold and worth."

With this, Jeremiah began to lose his firm grip on the here and now, lightly floating downward, riding a slide of ruby waves. He soon found steadfastness, on a ground that floated salt water and echoed a drone of tiresome weeping. Focusing his mind to see more clearly, Jeremiah became captivated by a giant, pitiful beauty, who sat on her heels, bending forward and shielding her fountains of sorrow. A thick, satin, blue cloth, hung about her waist as though a dumb witness to her wailing. Sympathetically dripping from her mothering cups, he could see the flowing milk of her understanding. It swam into her salty stream of emotion, was fortified with love, became churned by goodwill, and then manifested itself in crisp white lilies.

Suddenly she threw back her head, swaying waist-length ruby hair about her, and opened her mouth, letting a yawn drag itself from her solar plexus. She seemed unaware that Jeremiah stood watching as she displayed her routine of tired weeping and silent yawning. Jeremiah watched for as many yawns, he could resistance, until their eyes met in surprise, rendering them both silent and still.

Jeremiah hesitantly nodded his head, tearing the stillness in preparation to speak. "What is your name?" His wide eyes waited for her reply.

Her voice, low yet soft, replied, "My name is Magdalene, born from the great eye of compassion."

He drank her voice as if excellent wine, and his thirst questioned her further. "Magdalene, why do you cry?"

With more tears, she answered, "My tears are the weeping for the ignorant. For they know not to cry for themselves. Those who cry with fear, hate or lost sadness often create tears in the astrals. I purify them by crying them away with love."

Empathy towards her duty moved Jeremiah's feet a little nearer, as he asked, "But what of your yawning? When will you cease?"

She answered through a yawn, "My yawning is their silent cries for help. My crying will cease when all are liberated and live according to the will of the highest mind. The element air is a major cleaner. Know that I am the well in which to empty."

Jeremiah fell to his knees in the presence of such a humble soul, and immediately understood the task that lay before him. For in his coat were many pockets filled with the winds of liberty; truths enough to peel off the masks of ignorance, such as possessiveness in the name of love, sentimentality worn as compassion and self-centredness instead of true self-awareness. Now understanding the message by the waters of St Justin,

Jeremiah's goodwill set sail his little ship of aspiration on the seas of accomplishment.

* * *

It was on a cold winter's morning that a small child gripped tight to a windowsill. Past the patterned curtains she could see the grey concrete yard was shiny with the hard rainfall. Her ears and heart experienced each pitter-patter of the moment. Quick on the scene flew a winged, feathered messenger. Landing softly with stick legs near a puddle, its small, bright eyes caught sight of the slight human frame and, although fast pelted by the maddening raindrops, it stood upright and strong. This good breath on wings inhaled winds of liberty and slowly exhaled into song.

As the girl leant forward, resting her warm forehead on the chilly windowpane, her wide, innocent eyes declared a motive of comfort and rescue. As total concentration ate each note of musical truth, her inner spirit touched lighter upon the ground, rendering her mesmerised, beyond any known dream. Her soul expanded fuller to pulse with each note of unfolding enchantment, evaporating her physical awareness.

Within her new-grown space formed an atmosphere of unlimited peace, existing steady and real. The correct motive of everything carouselled around her and, led by a silver thread, entered her higher being. The answer to everything gelled and became one in glowing, sweet harmony. Standing in complete stillness, her lungs breathed in the natural rhythm of majesty, as it showed her spirit that herself, the winged messenger and the song were one and the same.

EARTH

His eyes drank the scene around him, filling up and over the cup of appreciation. Far-reaching views of fields lay all about, ripening juicy green or golden crisp. Wildlife darted and chased just out of his focus, claiming more attention to detail. As the smell of freshly burrowed soil and sticky new shoots hung in the early morning air, he watched tiny dust particles dancing in a ray of sunlight, falling gently down, until a west wind shattered it into pieces, leaving it dripping through a cradle of leaves, uninjured but a fragment of its former glorious self.

Jeremiah spread out his consciousness thin to fill up his occupying space, discovering his new morphic form was a tough oak in early spring. By now he had realised that the thought was the deed, so within no space or time his singing companion stepped out from behind the veil, saying, "Your strength of character has found a fitting suit! Question not how you can journey or discover rooted and mute. Remember all that you will need shall pass by or be within easy reach. Trees are both spectators and participants."

With these words echoing away, Jeremiah felt alone again.

Just then, a language that tingled circled around him, itching his rough skin. For the next few moments, patience tried hard to translate, whilst intolerance just pointed to scratch, and, all too soon, understanding was thrown out as litter. "That's it! I have had enough! I don't understand. It just feels like a talk of rubbish."

Hearing his words out loud, an elastic realisation pinged him on the knotted nose. The nursing hand of understanding soon began to wrap the bandage of tree talk around his weeping need to know. After which he became attentive to all the talk in the forest. He smiled to hear the creaking dry talk of the sycamore return politeness to the fir's endless talk of immortality, and boasts of bravery by the smaller oaks to the elm that argued the importance of justice.

Suddenly, one of his exposed roots felt a thud. Calmly he brought his attention downwards to a knee-high whirlwind that spun faster and faster, until it created a mini soil-storm. Then, as quickly as it had spun, it stopped, revealing a little man sporting the cheeriest colours plus a funny little hat. He stood with one arm tucked under the other and his short, sturdy legs wide apart. Jeremiah deduced by his stance that he was going to demand some sort of explanation as to why a person energy was in a tree.

"What are you doing in a tree?"

Jeremiah's surprise snapped a few of his twigs. Not wanting to keep this stern character waiting for an answer, he quickly replied, "I am on a journey of discovery."

Upon this, the little man pitched in, "Yes, but of what?"

Jeremiah felt that the conversation could border along the lines of rudeness, so very politely informed him, "To gain some spiritual insight and collect rewards for my virtues." Jeremiah sent him a vibration smile, hoping to unfold his arms at least.

"I know why you're here. I just wondered if it was all that clear to you. Oh, by the way, I'm Maraz, an elemental. I've been given the job of welcoming you to our world," he said, pleased with himself as he jigged.

Jeremiah became bemused yet delighted, although he showed neither to Maraz. Instead he sought to trick the cheeky gnome into delivering further information by giving him the opportunity to puff up with self-importance, stating, "I suppose, you have also been given the important job of telling me a clue of some sort."

The gnome paused his fidgety dancing, took in a deep breath, and then exhaled a self-created spontaneous clue. "Well, you have toes to be wiggled and a head to be patted." Pleased with himself once again, he about-turned and skipped away, repeating his words with wiggles and giggles.

Jeremiah's lofty mind began to think of his many toes buried deep in the rich sod. Governed by the human instinct of desire leading willpower, he soon dived into the dark dirt between his wooden toes. Delving further, wearing only a mask of thin oak, he thrust his way through layers of dead seasons. Dreary felt the journey, tunnelling through the parasite-ridden darkness, so he anchored his emotions to the memory that truly he belonged to a land of sunlight and free movement. By now his reaching felt like falling, yet he felt safe and secure in a pocket of intuition that he was going to meet earth's sweet reason.

Suddenly, his falling felt like a subtle pulling. He

acknowledged this as a welcome, so lifted his heart with a warm, open greeting. Invisible movements around him seemed to quicken with a purpose. A new motive was lying all around him; surely its reason lay just ahead. Sure enough, as though a door to light had just swung open, he entered a clear space filled with light.

Jeremiah's mental eyes prised open wider, then clung fast to a lustrous scene before him, as standing ahead was a circle of five planetary lords. As tall as trees and as broad as walls, each was armed with a brilliant power of light. Shimmering with heavenly gold and polished with devotion, their eyes rested only nearly open, for they were constantly aware and working, creating a pulsing shield of protection around a most radiant sun caught in a solid sky, guarding a great She, who exists simply to nurture.

So intense was their brilliance that it burnt right through his emotional and mental strings, rendering him a puppet to her motive. He cried helplessly, unable to withstand the sight of her bleeding, open wounds, the very gashes from faulty humanity that is ignorant of her. Aware of the suckling before her, she tenderly drew Jeremiah to her burning breast, simply because she could not help herself. Here Jeremiah lay, wrapped in a thermal heaven that constantly gave, yet repeated, a vibration of gratitude. The scales of Jeremiah's reasoning crumbled. Through her language of abstract ripples, stately yet so delicate upon its delivery, the explanation of her gratitude waved. "Because, I am of service."

Time lay with contentment, until it was Jeremiah's time to return. The root he rode towards was the root he rode from. Returned replenished and connected, he felt reborn and unable to distinguish between his own pulse and that of the great She.

Up high once again, looking out across the fields, Jeremiah started meditating on the evening sun over the quiet far meadow. But he was interrupted, for work had found a rhythm as it tapped and danced around his bold trunk. A feast of fairies and botanic builders worked pushing and shifting stale energies, creating spaces for new growth.

In the midst of all this was Maraz, instructing eighty-foot Jeremiah, "Come on now, let's get to work. Make sure you pump up an even amount of energy, nice and slow."

Instantly knowing what to do, Jeremiah wrapped obliging thoughts around his roots, then began to breathe from the eminent She. He watched the energies work harmoniously with wands, cups, swords and pentacles, according to the architectural design, until the sounds of the countryside followed the sun over the hill and a coronation of knights, queens, kings and pages declared their work complete, leaving a banner of hush over the land.

Jeremiah felt the brothers, peace and solitude, greet one another within his solar plexus. Acknowledging this as a moment ripe for further insight, he closed his eyes to all about and drew all of his mind's energies together at the main branch to the west. His awareness grew taller and wider, at which point a will stronger than his own collected him. With this, images of his time with water floated before him. Just then, his singing companion sang, "Grace accepts many differences, of why and how others are."

As the pictures of his mind rolled away, the higher will took him to the south. Tears came to his young eyes, as a warm memory of his time with fire came to his mind. And again the singing voice spoke. "To serve others magnanimously is noble."

As the pictures of his mind rolled away again, the

higher will took him to the east. He inhaled a fresh breath of air and exhaled a memory from his time with air. Again the singing voice spoke. "Freedom is the spirit's liberty."

As these pictures of his mind rolled away once more, the higher will took him to the north. A grounding memory came to his mind and showed him a memory with earth. The singing voice spoke. "Humility flows, discriminating against none."

THE VISION

Jeremiah wept hard and fast into his hands, emotionally unqualified for such a celebration. All about him became a swirling pool of his own tears, which whirled him down a quantum tunnel, to land with a thud on shady grass, tasting the sweet air of his homeland. His docile mind bade his bones to do the same. But drained and not ready for sleep, he waded across the warm glade to a running stream of cool, crystal waters, to obey his dry, demanding tongue.

Rejuvenated and ready for a challenge, he climbed an immense boulder nearby. Endurance tested, the last of his triumphant breath burst from his lungs as he reached its gusty heights. As memories of his recent past misted over his here and now, inspiration captured the dove of gratitude, then set it free upon the winds of prayer. "Above me is a sovereign of the skies. Beneath me a divine pathway of pardon. Before me a privilege of indulgence. Beside me a prevailing motive. For I am truly blessed."

Then, all at once, the gigantic rock beneath him rumbled, the sky packed the clouds away and all above became a stage. For being born before him was a divine vision, and unfolding in its gliding, unfurling with clarity, were the faces of all his recent companions, each resonating a unique note, clear in pitch and tone.

Framing the vision were four archangels. First, he beheld a glorious sight, for standing majestically loving with long, flowing robes of green and a halo of golden light was archangel Gabriel, the guardian of water, smiling soft as his long, wavy hair hung around his shoulders, rippling as though the sea breezed through it. His features were strong and defined and his heart waved to Jeremiah's grace. His layers of long, flowing robes came alive with a treasure of tiny golden fish that weaved in and out of its swaying folds. As he leant towards young Jeremiah, a robin redbreast landed upon his shoulder. The archangel touched his head, blessed him for his virtue, then furnished him with a golden medal.

Then came the magnificent archangel Michael, the guardian of fire, standing bold and brave in robes aflame with yellow and a halo of golden light. His laughter roared with joy to see Jeremiah, bouncing his long curls of red hair about his shoulders, as though fire popped and cracked it so. His features were strong and defined and his heart melted to Jeremiah's nobleness. The layers of his flowing robes began to shift and unfold with the perfume of a thousand blooms. And there he saw Scentina, curled up on a rose. She kissed the palm of her chubby hand and blew it over to Jeremiah's. Kneeling beside the angel, basking in his glow, was the hard-working maid, whispering her many blessings. Archangel Michael leant towards young Jeremiah, touched his head, blessed him for his virtue, and then pinned a rose of solid silver to his heart.

As Jeremiah clutched his rewards with tears in his eyes, the beautiful archangel Raphael, the guardian of air, came before him, standing graceful and calm in robes of sky blue and a halo of golden light, and gazing under-standingly, with hair and eyes dark, yet as bright as a beacon to safety. His features were strong and defined and his heart was alight to Jeremiah's liberty. The layers of his flowing robes breezed about him like a song. Around his feet were ripples of ruby hair from the giant Magdalene, who tossed her hair back as she delivered a tear of liberty from her big, brown, shiny eyes. And all the while a blackbird sang, simply because it was free. Archangel Raphael, leant towards young Jeremiah, touched his head, blessed him for his virtue, and then placed in his hand a crisp white lily.

Next came Archangel Uriel, the guardian of earth, standing tall and robust in robes of scarlet red and a halo of golden light. His eyes were filled to the brim with hope and mercy, framed by strong, straight hair. His features were bold and defined and his heart was rooted to Jeremiah's humility. The layers of his flowing robes sparkled like diamond dust captured by the light. Behind him shone the dazzling sun, emanating her constant giving, and around his feet was a circus of elementals, displaying their magic at work and led by a bossy ringmaster, Maraz. Archangel Uriel leant towards young Jeremiah, touched his head, blessed him for his virtue, and then placed at Jeremiah's feet a small, hard rock.

All the while, in the distance, he could see six figures watching without speaking. Five of them were the shining planetary lords, and the other one seemed strangely familiar - an old man in grey, with clothes just as tired as his face, yet with eyes that knew so much more.

All this became too much for Jeremiah, who from his emotions crumbled to meet the dusty stone. As he clasped his hands together tightly, a pledge to the divine flew from his heart and perched on his lips, to be spoken away on the wings of devotion. "I promise to live out my days according to the plan of the highest will."

After these words were spoken, the colossal boulder beneath him rumbled and the skies were sliced open by a hot, sharp blade of white lightning, melting the silver floor of heaven as it fell upon the earth. Each raindrop rang out a simple note of music and, falling harder, they erupted into an anthem that Jeremiah had come to know so well. Wishing to be saturated with the sound of majesty, happiness raised Jeremiah's face and arms to the skies, breaking the notes upon his skin and melting the song right through him. As Jeremiah's soul hummed, its musical existence unfolded all around him, showing how it played around the trees, echoed through the valleys, cut into stones and led the fields on fire to dance with flighty rhythm.

In the midst of all this majesty, a familiar voice harmonised. "I am many notes to many ears. I am the piercing shrill in the poor mind's rest, yet the symphony of a rich mind at work. Each soul should seek to attune, and be of service - an instrument, of my orchestra."

As this singing echoed into the distance, Jeremiah climbed down from the gigantic boulder and, taking hold of an axe a soul put by for this purpose, he began to break the giant stone into many parts. Many suns and moons had passed to the music of his axe by the time that Jeremiah gathered the mountain of stone and started to construct them into a bridge over the rushing stream. Many tides later, he pulled himself out of deep, musical concentration to see the bridge complete.

Again, his humane heart gave instructions. So, taking hold of the small, hard rock, he fixed it to the mantel of the bridge. Then he freely gave the white lily to a wing of liberty. Nobly he sacrificed his silver rose to the campfire, and gracefully set sail downstream a leaf, housing the golden medal. But, as Jeremiah glanced into the lucid water, it reflected a tale of an old, bearded man, whose clothes and face were worn, yet whose eyes knew so much more. With this, he knew it was time to tread the bridge of no return. His frail feet balanced his crooked spine up and over the bridge of humility.

A melodious song sang from his heart a tune he knew

so well. "By the purposeful will of grace, just be. By the goodwill of nobleness, just serve. By the unconditional will of liberty, just know. By the willpower of humility, just experience."

As his words harmonised with a heavenly choir, he saw the evidence to the next part in the plan, as the fine golden quill of his creator beckoned him on, then point to his place in the orchestra.

The Author's Website:

www.psychicmediumreadings.co.uk